VAMPIRE VACATION

Adapted by Maureen Spurgeon from
original Cosgrove Hall Productions
script by Peter Richard Reeves
and directed by Chris Randall.

Carnival
An imprint of the Children's Division
of the Collins Publishing Group
8 Grafton Street, London W1X 3LA

Published by Carnival 1988

Reprinted 1989

Count Duckula is a registered trademark of
THAMES TELEVISION plc.
Copyright © COSGROVE HALL PRODUCTIONS 1987

ISBN 0 00 194471 1

Printed & bound in Great Britain by
PURNELL BOOK PRODUCTION LIMITED
A MEMBER OF BPCC plc

Deep in the heart of Transylvania, it seemed as if the rain would never stop. Water trickled down walls, dripped through ceilings and plopped into a collection of buckets and bowls in a symphony of dismal-sounding clangs which echoed right through to the dungeons of Castle Duckula.

Thunder rolled . . . Lightning flashed around the black skies . . . And if any visitor had been foolish enough to knock at the great oak door for shelter, saying something like: "Nice weather for ducks!" Count Duckula would have probably snapped his beak and hit them with his broccoli sandwiches.

Even a polite knock at the door sounded like a soggy cheeseburger wrapped in blotting paper.

"Enter!" Duckula called out wearily. Next minute, he wished he hadn't bothered. Seeing his manservant, Igor, being swept into the room in a torrent of water was not a pleasant sight – even for the latest in a long line of vampire ducks.

"Good morning, Sir," droned Igor, not seeming to mind the wet. "And isn't it all so delightfully gloomy, Sir? The chains in the dungeons are rusting very nicely . . ."

Duckula, however, was far more interested in the drink Igor had brought him.

"Ah!" he cried, reaching out for the tray, and cheering up considerably. "Carrot juice! My favourite vegetarian treat!"

That was his second mistake in one morning.

"Yuucch!" He had never tasted anything quite so awful. "That's not carrot juice!"

"No, Milord," agreed Igor, with a respectful bow. "It is, in fact, a Vintage 1963 Yugoslavian Blue Blood . . ."

"Aaaagh!" Duckula screamed again, grabbing at his throat, then diving into all the puddles he could find before tipping up the coal bucket and gulping down every drop of rainwater inside. Anything to get rid of that dreadful taste in his mouth!

Igor looked on with some satisfaction. All too often he thought that Count Duckula was not really his idea of an evil, wicked, blood-sucking vampire, brought back to life every hundred years.

"I agree it is a little heady, Sir. Nevertheless, an extremely good year!"

Just then there came another voice, followed by the sound of big feet padding along the hall outside.

"Coo-ee, Duckyboos! Nanny's coming!"

Count Duckula gave another yell.

"Oh, no! Quick, Igor – open the . . ."

Too late! Nanny never could seem to manage the art of opening doors – which was just one reason why she always had to go around with one arm in a sling.

So Count Duckula and Igor weren't too surprised when she burst into the room on another tidal wave, bringing the door with her.

"You know," she quavered, as both she and the door drifted towards them, "it's a bit damp in the hall!"

This was too much for Count Duckula.

"Igor," he growled, "how can we get away from this dreadful Transylvanian drizzle?"

Igor bowed again. "Perhaps Spain, Milord?"

"Don't they have any rain there?"

"Mainly on the plain, Sir . . ."

"Well, that won't worry us! We'll go by castle as usual, eh? Heh-heh! Mainly on the plain, you said, Igor! Plain – aeroplane! But we're going by our own travelling Castle Duckula! Get it, Igor? Get it?"

"Unfortunately, yes, sir," Igor responded coldly, and turned away, twirling a model of the globe with one bony finger. "The Duckulas have always found a warm welcome in Spain, sir, at your cousin Don Diego's . . ."

"Warm welcome, eh?" Duckula was brightening up by the minute. "Friendly kind of guy, huh?"

"No, sir. A pyromaniac . . ."

"Oooh!" Nanny drew in her breath. "He's nothing of the sort, Mister Igor. He just likes setting fire to things!"

"Spain . . ." mused Duckula thoughtfully, spinning the globe so hard that it burnt his hand! "Ow, that is hot! Just what we all need!"

He began scampering around, his black vampire's cloak billowing behind him. "Pack my broccoli sandwiches, Nanny! We're off on our holidays!"

Nanny was delighted.

"Ooh, I loves holidays! I'm so happy, Mister Igor, I could give you a hug!"

"No . . . No, Nanny," begged Igor. "Please, Nanny, I . . . Aaagh . . . !"

His screams were even heard by Von Goosewing, the bumbling old vampire catcher, whirling about overhead in his ancient balloon.

"Someone in trouble at Castle Dugula?" he croaked. "Then, I, ze great Doctor Von Goosewing must save them!"

He drew out the stake which he always kept handy, ready to plunge into the heart of any vampire who happened to be passing – and plunged it straight into the balloon instead!

There was a loud hiss, then the balloon began spinning madly through the sky before flopping down behind some trees – almost at the very same moment as a flash of lightning lit up a sign which read:

SECRET TUNNEL TO CASTLE DUCKULA. PLEASE KEEP TO THE LEFT.

"Zo!" cried Von Goosewing. "Ve shall enter ze castle from ze underneath! Now . . . what I do wiz ze vampireometer?"

Meanwhile, Count Duckula was already looking forward to his sunshine holiday.

"Spain! I can't wait!" he whooped, taking a running jump into his favourite coffin which would launch Castle Duckula on its travels. "Espana, then! And step on it!"

The stormy Transylvanian sky suddenly lit up, streaked with bright red and yellow flashes. Castle Duckula shot up into the air in a cloud of smoke and dust, which only cleared when Duckula stepped out of the coffin again – this time wearing a pair of goggles and a snorkel, and carrying a deck-chair and surfboard.

"Ah! Wonderful Spain!" he cried, sniffing the air eagerly. "Can't wait to get out there in that sunshine!"

"Boy . . ." came another voice, and one of the flagstones creaked alarmingly. "That's some tunnel! Hey you! Have you seen a vampire around here?" Goosewing hadn't recognised Duckula in his beach outfit.

"Goosewing!" groaned Duckula. "What are you doing in Spain?"

"Spain?" Goosewing echoed blankly, lifting the flagstone a little higher and looking all around. "I must have taken the wrong turning somewhere! Please excuse me . . . I am so sorry . . ."

The flagstone slammed down, but Count Duckula didn't even look round. He was too busy breathing in the warm Spanish air.

"Down to the beach at once!" he declared approvingly, then took another sniff. "Hey – smells like Nanny's burnt the dinner again! I wonder what we're having?"

He sniffed again. "Ah, yes! Curtains! Then he thought again. "Funny . . . We don't usually have curtains on a Tuesday."

It was then the truth dawned on him. His fire-loving cousin Don Diego had already been up to his tricks!

"Help! shrieked Duckula, desperately trying to blow out the flames leaping up all around him. "Help! Fire, fire! Aaaagh!"

Panic-stricken, he darted towards a wash basin full of water dripping from a leaky tap, scooping up as much as he could carry in his two big yellow hands. Too bad it wasn't enough to dampen more than a little crackle!

"Help!" he yelled again, managing to toss the flaming hem of his vampire's cloak into the water just in time. "Fire! Fire!"

"Don't worry, my little Duckyboos!" quavered Nanny, arriving on the scene and reaching out towards the wash basin with her one good arm. "Nanny's here! She knows what to do!"

"No, Nanny!" screamed Duckula in horror. "Nanny, wait! Not that!"

But it was no good. With just half a tug, the wash basin was wrenched away from the wall, and gallons of water began gushing out, swirling all around Castle Duckula.

"Flooded out again!" wailed Duckula, as he and Nanny floated down the hall. I thought we came to Spain to get away from it all!"

Still the water came pouring out, filling the whole of Castle Duckula, until, in the end, the great front door burst open, and they were all swept out together on a tidal wave!

It all happened so quickly, that nobody noticed they were heading straight towards a huge, burning haystack – not until the rush of water had put out the fire in one enormous sizzle, and Duckula, Igor and Nanny landed on the ground in a soggy heap.

"So!" boomed out a deep voice. "Who is zis that puts out our fun fire?"

"Oooh!" squealed Nanny, her beady eyes lighting up. "I loves a fun fair! All them swings and roundabouts!"

Anyone could see that Don Diego's Bandit-in-Chief wasn't very impressed.

"What is she talking about?"

"Take no notice!" gabbled Count Duckula. "It – it's just that we – we forgot to turn right at the roundabout, and . . . goodness, is that the time?" He hoped the bandit wouldn't notice that he wasn't wearing a watch. "Come along you two, or we'll miss the – the . . . We'll miss the . . ."

"Coconuts!" finished Nanny, looking very pleased with herself.

"Coconuts?" echoed Duckula in amazement.

"Coconuts?" thundered the bandit.

"I always miss the coconuts on the Coconut Shy!" explained Nanny patiently.

"The only thing she wouldn't miss," sighed Duckula, "is her head!"

The bandit gave a sinister snarl. "I would be happy to make arrangements," he said.

"How wonderful to grovel before a man of such intellect, such sensitivity . . ." broke in Igor, hands clasped together in deep respect.

"Igor!" Duckula gave a horrified gulp. "I don't really want Nanny without her head!"

"Why ever not, Sir?"

"Well – she wouldn't be able to see where she was going . . ."

"So, Milord?"

"Well . . . she might bump into things!"

It seemed quite a good joke at the time. Funny enough to make even Igor enjoy a rare chuckle. But it was clear Don Diego's bandit had no sense of humour.

In a matter of moments, Nanny, Igor and Count Duckula were put into chains and thrust upside down into cages for everyone to see.

"Ladies and gentlemen!" proclaimed the bandit. "May I present His Honourable Highness, the Dirty, Diabolical, Dastardly and Disgusting – Don Diego!"

There was a blinding flash, then a loud bang which made everyone jump . . . and Don Diego emerged from a cloud of dust, coughing madly.

"I – I must cut down from forty explosions a day," he spluttered. "It – it's ruining my health!"

"Oh, Don Diego, Sir," said Igor, sounding quite polite for someone standing on his head. "May I introduce your Transylvanian cousin, Count Duckula?"

"Count Duckula?" screeched Don Diego. "Why didn't you say so? Release them at once! Take them to the great hall in my castle!"

Igor thought this sounded a whole lot better than being chained up in cages. And, as he and Nanny watched from the shadows, it did seem as if Don Diego meant to be quite friendly . . .

"Humble apologies, my dear Count Duckula!" he was saying, a big smile on his thin, ugly face. "You okay, now?"

"No, I am not, Cousin!" Duckula snapped, still in a bad temper. "You set fire to my castle – remember? You must be crazy!"

"No, no!" Don Diego insisted. "Only half crazy!" He grabbed Duckula's arm. "Did you hear something, Cousin?"

"No . . ."

Don Diego began flitting around, darting in and out of all the doorways and arches.

"They are everywhere, watching me . . . All of them hate me . . ."

"Hate you? All of them?"

"Si. Just because I tall and handsome and strong and good and kind . . . And because I chop some villagers into little pieces now and again . . . Ha-ha-ha!" There was a menacing glint of his sharp, white fangs. "And the really fat ones – I save them for tonight's fiesta for the vampires from all over Spain!"

There was a horrified pause, with Igor and Nanny struggling to hold their breath in the background. Then, Count Duckula stuck out his yellow beak.

"No! No, I cannot let you chop people up, Don Diego! What's more, I will do anything to stop you!"

"Anything?" Don Diego was definitely interested, his bloodshot eyes gleaming expectantly.

"Anything!"

The vampire's next remark made Igor cover his eyes in despair.

"Then, tonight, you fight the most horrible bull in all Spain, El Loco! His name means The Mad One! You understand?"

Still Count Duckula stood firm, arms folded across his skinny chest.

"I'm not afraid of you, Don Diego! Nor this El Loco of yours! Till tonight, then!"

Nanny felt quite proud that Count Duckula sounded so brave. But once Don Diego had flitted out of sight, his evil laughter echoing behind him, Count Duckula gave such a scream, clutching at Nanny's apron and falling to his knees.

"Aaaagh! Nanny! Nanny, I'm going to die! Help,

help!"

"Oh, Mister Igor!" wailed Nanny. "We can't let anything happen to my darling duck!"

"Hey!" called out a voice they all knew only too well, and Von Goosewing emerged through the gloom, complete with a very crumpled map. "Fritz – you know the way back to Transylvania?"

"I believe the underground is very reliable, Sir," replied Igor, and, with a commendable sense of duty, lifted the nearest flagstone and pushed Von Goosewing out of sight!

Now, he felt, he could really concentrate on helping Count Duckula fight the fiercest bull in the whole of Spain . . . even though, as the manservant for hundreds of years to a long line of terrible vampire ducks, he quite enjoyed all the horrible bits.

Nanny, however, had other views.

"Well, I don't think it's right!" she told Duckula, chins wobbling most indignantly. "You don't want to go around being silly and acting the goat!"

For a moment, Igor's gloomy-looking face actually beamed with excitement.

"Nanny, that's it! Acting the goat! Or, rather – the bull!"

"Huh?" quacked Duckula. "What do you mean, Igor?"

"Nanny, sir! We dress her up as a bull, and you fight her! She's big enough!"

"Are you saying I'm fat, Mister Igor?" queried Nanny.

"Yes, Nanny."

"Oh . . ." Nanny paused to consider. "Well – that's all right, then . . ."

"But, won't they notice, Igor?" asked Duckula, thinking it was just as well to attend to all the little details.

"Not if you were to distract them, sir!" responded Igor, becoming quite enthusiastic about the whole idea. "Why, you could change into a vampire bat, and sink your fangs into a few necks!"

"Even better, I could sing a few songs!" Duckula interrupted eagerly. "Ride a bike. Play my banjo!"

"Come, Nanny," said Igor, somewhat hurriedly. "Time to put our plan into action . . ."

Before long, all the leading vampires were taking their seats around the bullring ready for the big fight.

"What a wonderful night!" Don Diego kept saying. "On a night like this, I could burn down half of Spain!"

He would have been even more delighted to see Nanny fussing around Count Duckula in his matador's costume.

"Master Duckula," she sighed, "I haven't seen you looking so nice since you had those photographs taken in your romper suit!"

"That was very embarrassing, Nanny!" Duckula snapped. "Especially when I was seventeen and a half at the time!"

"Come, Nanny," Igor broke in, holding out an old curtain with a swishy-looking black tail and a pair of horns which looked suspiciously like the handlebars from Duckula's bicycle. "Time for you to change!"

And, very calmly, he led her away to a backstage room, ushering her gently inside like the perfect gentleman he was – completely ignoring the stamping and the bellowing which came from the next stable, and where the name "EL LOCO" appeared above the door.

Duckula was quite looking forward to being a star.

"Time for my performance, Igor!" he announced.
"Where's Nanny?"

"In the changing room, Sir. I'll let her out . . ."

He went and lifted up a huge wooden bolt, looking up
just long enough to read the name over the door . . .

His droopy-looking eyes widened in terror. There was
a volley of deafening snorts, a blast of fiery, steaming
breath, and two giant horns thrust back the door,
flattening Igor against the wall.

The Count was most impressed.

"Wow! Wow-ee-wow, Nanny! Anyone would think
you were a real bull!"

This didn't please El Loco at all, his red eyes blazing fire and steam coming out of both nostrils.

"All right, don't get carried away!" Duckula prattled on. "Hear that fanfare? That's our music!" And he held out his matador's cape for good measure. "Let's go!"

But El Loco was already heading straight to the centre of the bullring, trampling over Count Duckula in the process!

"Watch it, Nanny!" yelled Duckula, scrambling to his feet and reaching for his bicycle. "I am the star, you know!"

Everyone agreed, it was quite a sight watching Duckula chasing El Loco on his bike, singing and playing his banjo at the same time!

"Huh!" Don Diego snorted almost as loudly as the bull. "He's even nuttier than I am!"

He would have been even more surprised had he known that Von Goosewing was also there with his vampireometer, its lights flashing and the indicator pointing to one sign on the dial: VAMPIRE!

"Vampire!" shrieked Von Goosewing, whipping out his special stake-firing gun at once. "Vampire!"

Don Diego was so taken by surprise, he quite forgot himself and gave a blood-curdling scream . . .

"Quick, Nanny!" cried Igor, thinking it was Count Duckula, and struggling to let her out as fast as he could. "The young master needs you . . ."

Anything else he might have said was smothered by the door falling down on top of him. Playing the part of a bull with handlebar horns might not have won Nanny any acting awards – but nobody could deny she was a champion at breaking down doors!

"I'm coming, Duckyboos!" she yelled out. "Nanny's here!"

"Nanny?" echoed Duckula, both the bike and the banjo-playing screeching to a stop. "Then – wh-who's this?"

Duckula and El Loco stared at each other, the bull baring its huge teeth and pawing the ground.

"Aaaagh!" screamed Duckula, pedalling madly around the ring, haunted by the sight of two great eyes staring out of an enormous head – and that was before he even saw Igor!

"Out of the way, Igor!" bellowed Duckula – but Igor didn't stand a chance. Up he flew on to the front of the bike, with Duckula still pedalling furiously, closely followed by El Loco, then Nanny, just ahead of Don Diego (being chased by Von Goosewing with his vampireometer) and yelling out: "If I get my hands on you, in two minutes you are roast beef!"

But, whether he meant the bull or Nanny, nobody really knew . . .

Somehow, they managed to reach Castle Duckula, scrambling inside just in time for Count Duckula to leap into the coffin which would transport them safely back to Transylvania.

"Home at last!" the Count sighed with relief. "Thank goodness we got rid of that horrible bull!"

But, even as he spoke, the casle walls began rumbling with the loud snorting and bellowing which each of them knew only too well . . .

"El Loco!" shrieked Count Duckula. "Nanny! Igor! whose idea was it to spend a holiday in sunny Spain?"

The only answer was the ear-splitting din of running footsteps, screams and thundering hoofs echoing through Castle Duckula.

And after a fire and a flood, being captured by bandits, caged up in chains, taking on a mad bull AND dealing with boring Doctor Von Goosewing, they all agreed that a little Spanish sunshine went a long, long way. In fact, the further the better!

Ole!